My Teacher
Sleeps in School

P9-BZI-850

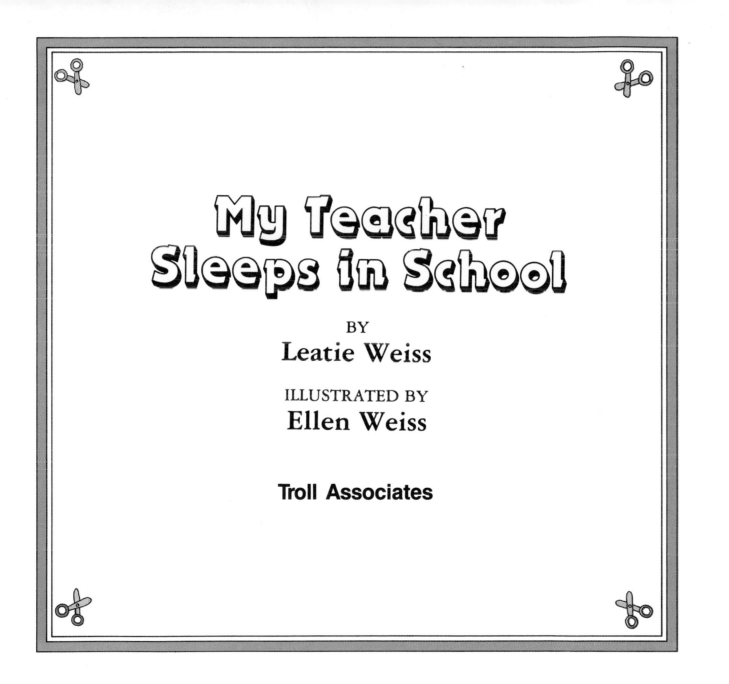

My Teacher Sleeps in School

BY
Leatie Weiss

ILLUSTRATED BY
Ellen Weiss

Troll Associates

To Gary, who always knows where teachers sleep,
and to all my students in Hawthorne, New Jersey,
who were never quite sure. —L.W.

To Katie, Susu, and Peter. —E.W.

PUFFIN BOOKS
A Division of Penguin Books USA Inc.
375 Hudson Street, New York, New York 10014
Penguin Book Ltd, 27 Wrights Lane, London W8 5TZ England
Penguin Books Australia Ltd, Ringwood, Victoria, Australia
Penguin Books Canada Ltd, 2801 John Street, Markham, Ontario, Canada L3R 1B4
Penguin Books (N.A.) Ltd, 182–190 Wairau Road, Auckland 10, New Zealand

Penguin Books Ltd, Registered Offices: Harmondsworth, Middlesex, England

First published by Frederick Warne & Co., Inc., 1984
Published in Picture Puffins 1985
Reprinted by arrangement with Viking Penguin, a division of Penguin Books USA Inc.

Text copyright © Leatie Weiss, 1984
Illustrations copyright © Ellen Weiss, 1984
All rights reserved

Manufactured in the United States of America

Set in Garamond

Library of Congress catalog card number: 85-40449
(CIP data available)
ISBN 0 14 050.559 8

Except in the United States of America, this book is sold subject to the condition
that it shall not, by way of trade or otherwise, be lent, re-sold, hired out, or
otherwise circulated without the publisher's prior consent in any form of binding
or cover other than that in which it is published and without a similar condition
including this condition being imposed on the subsequent purchaser

10 9 8 7 6 5 4 3 2 1

"Good-bye," called Mrs. Marsh. "I'll see you all tomorrow." Mrs. Marsh went back into the school, and everyone began walking home.

"I think the teacher sleeps in school," said Mollie. "I think she stays there all night long."

"What a dumb idea," said Gary. "Teachers don't sleep in school."

"Mrs. Marsh does," said Mollie. "She's always there when we come. And she's always there when we leave. I think the classroom is her house."

"Why don't you ask her?" dared Gary.

"I did once," said Mollie, "and she just laughed and laughed. But she didn't say yes or no."

"But where would she sleep?" said Gary. "Where would she eat?"

"Let's look around the room for clues tomorrow," said Mollie. "Maybe we'll find out."

The next day Gary could hardly do his work. He kept watching Mrs. Marsh and wondering. "What if it's really true?" he whispered to Mollie. "What if she really lives here?"

Pretty soon Lisa and Jason were wondering too.

"Where does she keep her clothes?" asked Jason.

"In the closet, of course," said Lisa. "Behind the paste and paper."

At play time, when Mrs. Marsh wasn't looking,
they opened the closet door.

"Look!" whispered Lisa. "A towel! And soap!"

"And a mirror!" squealed Gary.

"I'll bet she gets dressed in this closet," said Mollie.

"And *undressed*, too," giggled Lisa.

"I'll bet she wears funny pajamas," said Gary.
"And gloppy cream on her face," said Jason.
They pictured Mrs. Marsh in her pajamas and
couldn't stop laughing.

Next, they tiptoed over to the play kitchen.

"I saw her hide two bags here this morning," said Mollie.

"More proof!" said Gary in a loud whisper. "It's paper plates and napkins and lots of forks and spoons. She must be having company."

"I see cake mix and eggs in this bag," whispered Lisa. "She must be baking a real cake."

"I think she cooks her supper here every night," said Mollie.

"That oven is only make believe," said Jason.

"She can make it work," Mollie said. "Teachers can do *anything*."

Then they thought about where
Mrs. Marsh ate her supper,

and did her laundry,

and brushed her teeth
before she went to bed.

But where did she sleep? That was still a mystery.

"Maybe she sleeps on the bookshelf," suggested Gary.

"Or on the piano," said Mollie.

They looked and looked, but they couldn't find any clues.

Then after lunch, everyone was getting ready for an art project. When Mrs. Marsh was in the closet getting paper, Gary snooped around behind her desk.

"There's something under here!" he whispered. "Come and see!"

"A pair of slippers!" said Mollie. "And a pillow! She must sleep under her desk. We never thought of that!"

"I told you so," said Gary. "She really *does* sleep in school!"

"Poor Mrs. Marsh," sighed Lisa. "I bet it's lonely here at night."

"And creepy," said Jason.

Then Mollie had an idea. "Let's leave her a good-night snack," she said.

"And a nice note," said Jason.

"And something cuddly to sleep with," said Lisa.

Gary had part of a sandwich left over from lunch. Jason had saved six potato chips for later. Lisa got the teddy bear out of her cubby. Mollie was in charge of the note.

"Surprise!" she wrote. "We know you sleep
here. Good night—sleep tight."

Gary promised to keep everything a secret, but soon the
whole class knew. Everyone started giggling and whispering.
    Mrs. Marsh looked puzzled. "What is going on here
today?" she asked.
    But nobody answered.

By three o'clock, Mollie had wrapped up the good-night package. Then Gary sneaked it under Mrs. Marsh's desk.

The next day everyone got to school early. They could hardly wait to hear what Mrs. Marsh would say.

But all she said was, "We're going on a mystery trip today." And she wouldn't tell them where. Not even a hint.

Everyone got on the school bus.
They rode and rode.

At last they stopped at a
white house with a blue door.

"This is where I live," announced Mrs. Marsh.
Gary looked at Mollie. Mollie looked at Lisa. Lisa looked
at Jason. Then they followed Mrs. Marsh inside.

Mrs. Marsh showed them where she cooked her supper,

and did her laundry,

and brushed her teeth before she went to bed.

"And this," said Mrs. Marsh, "is where I sleep."
"Every night?" asked Mollie.
"Every night!" said Mrs. Marsh.
Then she showed them her children's rooms.

"You even have children?" asked Lisa.

"Yes," said Mrs. Marsh. "They're in school all day, just like you. When my husband and I get home from work, we're all together."

"Just like us!" said Mollie.

"Now follow me," said Mrs. Marsh. "I've saved the best for last."

She led the class into the dining room.
There were the paper plates and napkins
from the shopping bag at school!

"I've been planning this special treat for
the class," said Mrs. Marsh.

"Oh," said Mollie, "we thought . . ."

"I know what you thought," Mrs. Marsh
said, laughing.

Then Mrs. Marsh brought out a big cake,
and just like Mollie's note, it said "Surprise!"
"I baked this last night," said Mrs. Marsh.
"I baked it in my own oven, in my own
kitchen. And after that I went to sleep
in my own real bed."

Gary gave Mollie a poke. "I knew it all the time,"
he bragged. "Teachers *never* sleep in school!"
Mollie didn't even answer him.

Mrs. Marsh was smiling at her in a special way. "Mollie,"
she said, "would you help me cut the cake?"
Mrs. Marsh served everyone a piece with a heart on it.

And she saved the biggest heart for Mollie.